For Lisa
E. A. K.

For those of us who have naively stumbled,
and still found happiness.
R. S.

Library of Congress Cataloging-in-Publication Data
Kimmel, Eric A.
The Goose Girl : a story from the Brothers Grimm / retold by Eric
A. Kimmel ; illustrated by Robert Sauber.-- 1st ed.
p.   cm.
Summary: On her way to marry a distant prince, a young princess is
forced to trade places with her evil serving maid and becomes a
goose girl instead of a bride when she reaches her destination.
ISBN 0-8234-1074-9
[1. Fairy tales. 2. Folklore--Germany.] 1. Sauber Rob, ill.
II. Grimm, Jacob, 1785-1863. III. Grimm, Wilhelm, 1786-1859.
IV. Gänsemagd. V. Title.
PZ8.K527Go   1995   93-13138
398.21-dc20   CIP   AC
[E]

The GOOSE GIRL

A Story from the Brothers Grimm

Retold by Eric A. Kimmel

Illustrated by

Robert Sauber

Holiday House

New York

nce upon a time there was a queen who had a beautiful daughter, a princess so loving and kind that she rivaled the angels in heaven for goodness.

When the princess came of age, her mother betrothed her to a prince whose father ruled a distant kingdom.

The old queen prepared her daughter for the journey with great care. She packed a chest with beautiful clothes, exquisite presents, and rare trinkets, all made of silver and gold. Yet the queen never ceased to worry about her daughter. The princess had grown up surrounded by love. She had never heard a harsh word or seen a blow delivered in anger. She knew nothing of envy and hate. In her new home, far from her mother's protection, could she defend herself against those who might take advantage of her?

To provide for these concerns, the queen ordered her trusted serving maid Margaret to accompany her daughter on the journey. She gave the princess her own horse to ride. This horse, whose name was Falada, was no ordinary animal. Falada understood the language of human beings, and could speak it as well.

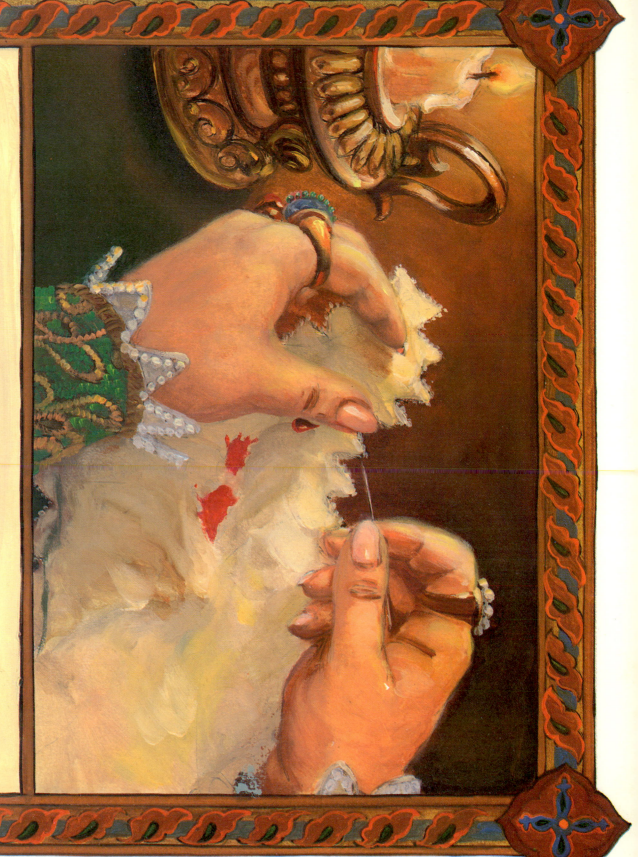

However, in spite of all her precautions, the queen could not rid herself of the fear that the journey would be an unfortunate one. When the time came for the queen to bid her daughter farewell, she pricked her thumb with a needle and let three drops of blood fall onto her linen handkerchief. She gave it to the princess, saying, "Beloved child, guard this well. Your mother's blood will watch over you and protect you." The princess tucked the handkerchief in her bodice. She kissed her mother good-bye and set out upon her journey.

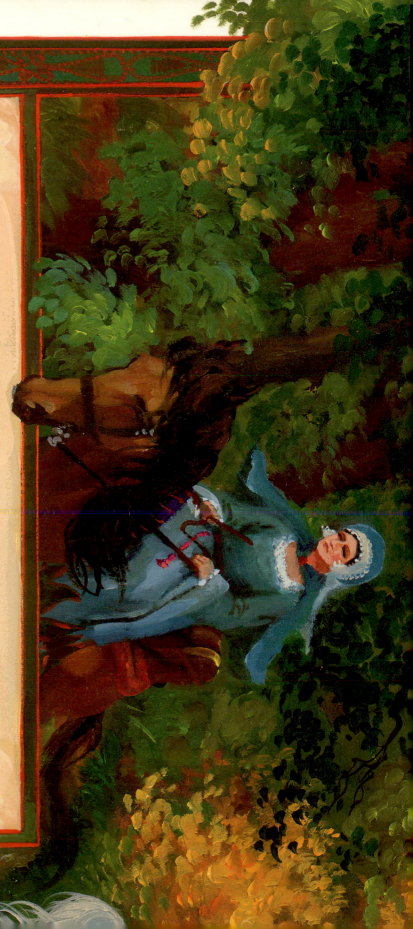

The princess and the serving maid rode out together. At noontime they came to a rushing stream. The sun beat down with great force, making the princess giddy.

"Sweet Margaret," she called to the serving maid, "fetch me a cup of cool water. My head pounds like a drum. I fear I will faint."

"Fetch it yourself," the maid answered rudely. "I am as hot as you are. Why should I serve you?"

Now the maid knew full well that had she dared utter such words in the presence of the queen, she would have been stripped of her clothes and lashed through the streets. However, the queen was far away and the princess, her daughter, was too kind and good-natured to properly rebuke her.

"Forgive me, Margaret. I did not mean to trouble you," the princess said. All by herself, she had to climb down from Falada, her horse, and kneel beside the stream to drink. Mud stained her lovely gown; sharp rocks tore its delicate fabric. "Heaven help me," the princess sighed in despair. Her good horse Falada turned his head and spoke:

"If your mother were to see,
Her heart would burst with grief for thee."

They continued on under a pitiless sun. Once more the heat made the princess faint. She begged for water. But Margaret answered with language so vile it made the princess weep for shame. Again, she had to climb down from her horse and kneel beside the muddy stream to drink. As she did so, the linen handkerchief with the three drops of her mother's blood slipped from her bodice and floated away. The moment Margaret saw that the princess had lost her protecting charm, her insolence knew no bounds. When the princess tried to remount Falada, Margaret pushed her aside.

"You don't need such a fine horse. My old jade will serve you better." Margaret then forced open the clothes chest. She selected the finest gown for herself. Flinging her servant's frock at the princess, she said, "Put that on. It suits you far better than it suits me." The princess, weeping, had to obey. The faithful horse Falada turned his head and replied,

"If your mother were to see,
Her heart would burst with grief for thee."

"She will never know. Nor will she hear a word of this." Margaret forced the princess to swear by God, the saints, and all the angels in heaven that she would never breathe a word of her maid's deceit to a living soul. But Falada saw everything and marked it in his memory.

With Margaret riding Falada and the princess astride Margaret's old jade, they traveled on until they reached the palace of the princess's bridegroom. The young prince came riding through the gate to meet them. He helped Margaret down from her horse and escorted her into the palace with great pomp and ceremony, for he assumed that she was his promised bride. He left his true bride, the real princess, standing alone in the courtyard.

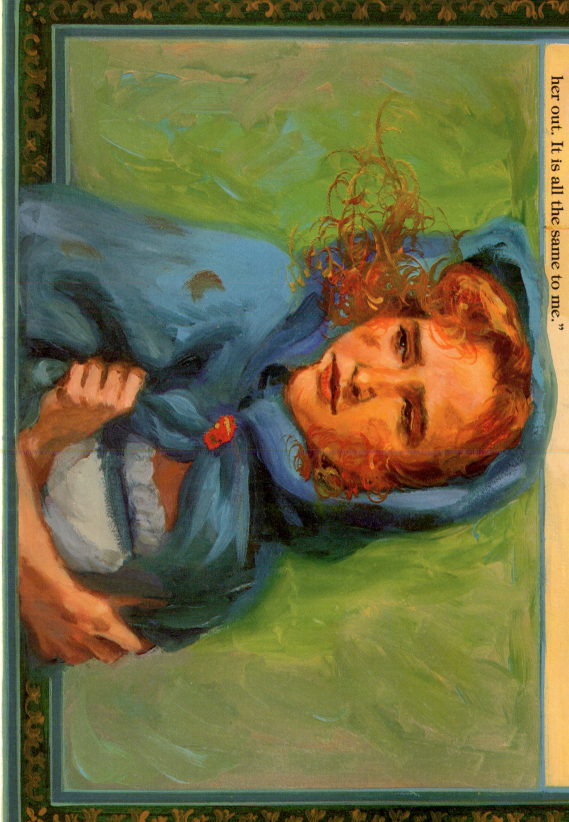

Now it so happened that the old king, the prince's father, happened to be looking down from a tower window. He noticed the young girl standing by herself, alone and forlorn.

"How lovely and delicate she is," he remarked to himself. "She does not resemble a servant at all. Were it not for her plain clothes and dirty face, I would swear that she was the true princess."

The king hurried downstairs to greet his new daughter-in-law. "Who is that girl in the courtyard?" he asked Margaret.

She replied, "A common slattern. I met her along the way, and feeling sorry for her, allowed her to accompany me. She is useless as a maidservant. Keep her, or throw her out. It is all the same to me."

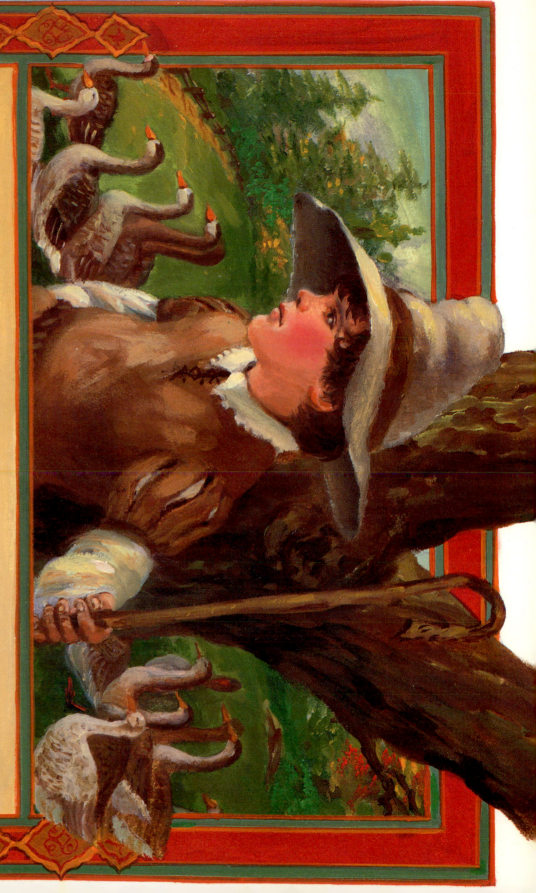

"I know something she can do," the king suggested. "We have a little boy, Conrad, who tends the geese. She can help him."

"Well and good, as long as I never have to see her," Margaret said. "However, now that I think about it, there is one favor you can grant me. Have my horse put down. He tried to throw me from his back. I will not tolerate such insolence."

Falada, of course, had done no such thing. Nonetheless, Margaret dared not let him live, for fear he would tell the truth about her.

And so noble Falada lost his life. The butcher bought his flesh and the tanner bought his hide. His head, which was of no use to anyone, was tossed on a rubbish heap. The princess found it there. She promised the butcher boy a whole month's wages if he would nail the head over the gate through which she and Conrad drove the geese each morning.

The next morning, when the flock came through the gate, the princess looked up at the horse's head and said in a voice tinged with sorrow,

"Alas, Falada, on the gate."

The head replied,

"Alas, queen's daughter, if your fate,
Your mother were to see,
Her heart would burst with grief for thee."

The princess and Conrad drove the geese to the meadow. As soon as the geese were settled in the grass, the princess untied the kerchief that bound her hair and began combing out her tresses. They sparkled in the sunlight like threads of pure gold. The little goose boy Conrad was so taken by the sight that he could not resist reaching out to pluck a few strands. The princess saw him stealing up behind her. Immediately she called out,

"Little Breeze, blow!
Conrad's hat, go!"

A breeze suddenly came up that blew Conrad's hat across the meadow. The boy ran after it, chasing it here and there. By the time he caught it, the princess had combed and braided her hair and tied it beneath her kerchief so that he could not get one single strand.

This happened day after day, until Conrad grew so angry he complained to the king.

"I won't herd geese anymore."

"Why not?" the king asked.

"That girl you gave me as a companion does nothing but vex me."

"What makes you say that?"

"Every morning when we drive the geese to the meadow," Conrad replied, "she stops beneath a dreary old horse's head hanging above the gate and says to it,

'Alas, Falada, on the gate.'

"The head answers,

'Alas, queen's daughter, if your fate,
Your mother were to see,
Her heart would burst with grief for thee.'

"Then, after we arrive at the meadow, she combs out her hair and says,

'Little Breeze, blow!
Conrad's hat, go!'

"The wind blows my hat away and I must chase after it. This happens every day. I want no more of it."

"How curious," the king exclaimed. He told Conrad to take the geese out one more time so he could see these events for himself. The king arose early the next morning and hid beside the gate. When Conrad and his companion herded the geese through, he saw the girl speak to the horse's head and heard the head answer, just as Conrad described:

"Alas, Falada, on the gate."

"Alas, queen's daughter, if your fate,
Your mother were to see,
Her heart would burst with grief for thee."

The king followed them to the meadow. When Conrad reached to pluck the girl's hair, she called forth a breeze that blew his hat away.

"Little Breeze, blow!
Conrad's hat, go!"

"Most curious. I wonder what it means," said the king. That evening he summoned the goose girl to his chamber. He described what he had seen that morning. He asked her why she did these things, and what they signified.

"I would gladly tell you, if I could," the goose girl answered. "But I have sworn an oath to heaven not to breathe a word to a living soul."

"Since that is the case," the king said, "why not tell your troubles to the iron stove standing in the corner? A stove is not alive, so you will not violate your oath."

As soon as the king left the room, the princess poured out her heart to the iron stove. She told the stove how Margaret, her serving maid, had abused and betrayed her, how she had usurped her rightful place and forced her to earn her living as a common goose girl.

"So!" said the king, standing at the door where he could hear every word. "It is just as I suspected. The goose girl is the true bride. The one who sits at my son's side and drinks from his cup is false."

That night at dinner the king said to Margaret, "An interesting case has come to my attention. I am uncertain how to decide it. Perhaps you can help."

"Of course," Margaret replied, flattered to be asked.

"A certain serving maid has broken her trust," the king continued. "She has abused her mistress, and worse, usurped her place. What should be done with her?"

Margaret replied without hesitation. "Here is what must be done. She should be put naked into a barrel lined with sharp spikes. Harness two white horses to the barrel. Let them drag it through the streets until she is dead."

"You have pronounced your fate. Let it be done," the king commanded. So cruel Margaret met her end.

Her glittering gown was given to the goose girl. From the moment she put it on, everyone recognized her as the true princess. She married the prince the next day. She never had to herd geese again and for the rest of her life lived happily ever after.